"Ugh!" Selena sighed as she flopped down on the couch next to her brother Jaden, "Eugene was SUPPOSED to be here already!" Jaden looks up from his homework, then squints, looking behind her. "What's that?" he said, pointing at a box on the table. "It has a card on top," he says as he grabs it, reading aloud: "Open me." Selena quickly snatched off the top, showing her brother what was inside, "Glasses... but they are super thick?" "Put them on," encouraged Jaden, as he put on the other pair. Selena cautiously placed them over her eyes.

A floating robot appeared before their eyes. "Hi, I'm Bot!" Selena slides her glasses off, and he disappears, so she slides them back on. Bot speaks again, "You can only see me when you have the glasses on because they allow you to see what we call 'Augmented Reality'. I'm not really in front of you, but the glasses let you see me." "Cool!" Selena and Jaden both exclaim.

"Do you want to go to where I live, the Metaverse?" Bot asks. "Yes!" they both respond quickly. A door appears in front of them and they walk through it.

Once they walk through the door, they see a virtual reality world. There are ice cream mountains, people running around with pickaxes and blocks, and even a parade of food wearing funny hats walking by them. The kids run to join in the parade.

Selina stares at the hats enviously, then turns to Bot, "I like their outfits more than what I'm wearing!". Bot tells them "While in the Metaverse you can change your clothing, let me show you how." He waves his arm and a menu appears with a lot of options. Selena points to a hat that suddenly appears on her head.

Jaden asks Bot, "What else can we do in the Metaverse?" "You can do lots of things like go shopping, see art called NFTs, watch videos of virtual influencers, and even play games!" Bot informed them.

Jaden decides he wants to play a racing game. Jaden selects a fast red sports car to race in. He comes in first place! Selena decides to enter the race on a unicorn with a rainbow tail.

Suddenly, Jaden and Selena hear a countdown coming from down the road. Bot yells "Hurry, or we'll miss the show!" As they arrive, they hear music start, and the singer grows in size so the whole crowd can see him. It's Selena's favorite singer. "S'mores Head!" Selena yells.
Everyone starts to dance.

Selena turns to Bot, "Can I buy his music?" Bot replies, "You need digital money called bitcoin if you want to buy things in the Metaverse." Selena asks, "How do I get bitcoin?" Bot shows them computers in a tunnel mining for it. One computer wipes sweat from his forehead, saying "This is hard work!" before it starts mining again. Bot says, "While I don't have a lot of bitcoin I do have just enough to buy the album for you."

Jaden says, "I'm exhausted from all the fun I've had, we've walked in a fruit parade, won a race, danced at a concert, used bitcoin, AND bought music. I think I need a nap!" Selena agrees, asking Bot, "Can we go home? I want to tell Eugene about all the cool things we've done today!"

Bot tells them, "You already are, just take off the glasses!" They do and are back home to see their best friend Eugene, who was also wearing the glasses. He was secretly Bot all along as an avatar! Jaden and Selena take a nap, dreaming about all the things they will do in the Metaverse tomorrow.

Virtual reality is the most empathetic technology ever created. It allows you to step into the shoes of someone else from a different walk of life, then see through their eyes. The Metaverse connects these experiences allowing a new generation to reach their vast potential.
-Eugene Capon II

Printed in Great Britain
by Amazon

83944506R10016